Kirch
E. Kramer
S. Campbell

P9-BIU-077

Adam Draws Hims...

Adam Draws Himself a Dragon

Irina Korschunow
translated from the German
by James Skofield
with pictures by Mary Rahn

A Harper Trophy Book
Harper & Row, Publishers

Adam Draws Himself a Dragon
First published in Germany by Deutscher Taschenbuch Verlag, Munich,
under the title *Hanno malt sich einen Drachen*.
Copyright © 1978 by Deutscher Taschenbuch Verlag GmbH & Co., KG
Translation copyright © 1986 by Harper & Row, Publishers, Inc.
Printed in the U.S.A. All rights reserved.

Library of Congress Cataloging-in-Publication Data
Korschunow, Irina.
    Adam draws himself a dragon.

    Translation of: Hanno malt sich einen Drachen.
    Summary: A young dragon comes to stay with Adam for
a while and they help each other overcome the problems
that make their school days unhappy.
    [1. Self-actualization (Psychology)—Fiction.
2. Schools—Fiction. 3. Dragons—Fiction]   I. Rahn,
Mary, ill.   II. Title.
PZ7.K8376Ad 1986   [E]   85-45256
ISBN 0-06-023249-8
ISBN 0-06-023252-8 (lib. bdg.)
    "A Harper Trophy book"
ISBN 0-06-440229-0 (pbk.)

First Harper Trophy edition, 1988

Contents

Adam Draws Himself a Dragon

1. Adam Is Alone

"Wake up, Adam," said Mother.

Slowly, very slowly, Adam crawled out of bed. Slowly, very slowly, he walked into the bathroom. He brushed his teeth and took his bath. Then he played boats with the soap dish.

"Hurry up, Adam!" called Mother. "Or you won't get to school on time."

On time! If Adam had his way, he would never go to school again. The other kids made fun of him because he was fat.

He had been looking forward to school at the beginning of fall, as he walked to school with his new book bag. But on the very first day, Larry Hall, who sat behind him, had called him "Greasy Gravy." And "Tuba-Tummy." Since then, Adam hated school. But his mother made him go.

"Have fun, Adam," said Mother as she waved to him from the door.

Slowly, very slowly, Adam started walking. He walked across the street and through the park. He walked through the school yard and into his classroom.

"Here comes Greasy Gravy!" hollered Larry Hall and shoved Adam against a bench. Adam wished he could shove him back. Or at least kick him. But he didn't dare. He was sure that Larry was stronger, and he had many friends. Adam had no friend. He sat in his seat, so upset and unhappy he couldn't pay attention.

"It's your turn, Adam," said Mrs. Beck, the teacher.

Adam didn't hear her.

"Adam!" called Mrs. Beck, "Wake up! It's your turn to read."

Adam was so upset he stuttered and stumbled and mixed up all his letters. The other children began to laugh and Mrs. Beck said, "You cannot sleep all the time, Adam! That's what night is for."

Math wasn't any better for Adam, and when it came time for Art class, Adam didn't even *try* to paint a picture. I can't do it, he thought.

But worst of all was Gym. Everyone was faster than Adam and he never even got the ball.

"Greasy Gravy's fat, fat, *fat*, so bop him with a baseball bat!" yelled Larry Hall. Adam was so unhappy he never wanted to see school again.

2. The Little Dragon

Slowly, very slowly, Adam walked through the park toward home. He walked past the big beech tree, and sat down on a bench. He didn't even notice how cold it was. With a dry twig, he began to draw lines and circles and X's in the sand.

Suddenly a head poked out of one of the X's. A real, live head! It was a small black head with a red tongue and a nose. Out of the nose curled dark smoke.

"Hello," said the small black head to Adam. "What kind of a funny thing are *you*? I've never seen such a funny dragon before."

"Dragon?" asked Adam. "Me? I'm not a dragon. I'm a person!"

The small black head blew a wisp of cloud from his nose.

"A person?" he puffed. "You *are*? My grandmother used to tell me people stories. But she said they were only fairy tales. Are you really a person?"

"Yes," said Adam. "What are you?"

"Me?" The little black head waggled back and forth. "Don't you know?"

Adam stared as a stomach, a back with two wings, a long tail, and four thick claws popped out of the ground. The creature was black as coal and no bigger than a guinea pig.

"Are you . . . ?" stammered Adam.

"Of *course* I'm a dragon," puffed the small black dragon. "I came from down under. From Dragonland. A very long way away."

Adam squatted down to look at the little dragon up close. He had scaly skin and bright, black eyes. The little dragon looked quite friendly.

"Why did you come here?" asked Adam.

The little dragon looked around carefully. He leaned closer to Adam, and whispered, "I ran away."

"Why?" asked Adam.

"Because I'm so little. My wings are so tiny I can't fly. And I only have one head," puffed the little dragon.

"Is that bad?" asked Adam.

"It is if you're a dragon. Everyone else has three heads. They always make fun of me in school. That's why I ran away.

"Can I stay with you?" asked the little dragon. "I could live in that thing there. It's just my size."

"*That* is my book bag," said Adam. "I take it to school with me."

"School? Do people have school?" puffed the surprised little dragon.

Adam nodded. "Yes," he said sadly.

"I thought only dragons had to go to school," said the little dragon. "In our school we learn how to breathe fire—red with one head, yellow with another, and blue with the third head."

"But you only blow out *smoke*," said Adam.

"I've just *started* school," said the little dragon. "Besides, I only have one head. What do you learn in your school?"

"Reading and writing and math and painting and singing," said Adam. He didn't like talking about school.

"That sounds like fun!" puffed the little dragon. "Will you take me to your school?"

Adam didn't answer.

"Please take me," begged the little dragon.

"First we have to go home," said Adam. "It's cold and I'm freezing." He opened his book bag, and the little dragon jumped inside.

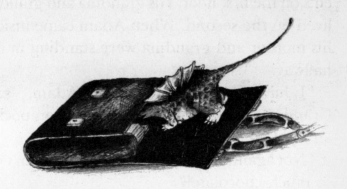

3. The Little Dragon Eats Chocolate Fire

The house where Adam lived was surrounded by a big, shady yard. Adam lived with his parents on the first floor. His grandma and grandpa lived on the second. When Adam came inside, his mother and grandma were standing in the hallway.

"I have something for you, Adam," said Grandma. She rummaged in her apron pocket and pulled out a large bar of chocolate.

"Not again!" cried Mother. "He shouldn't eat so much chocolate!"

"But he likes it!" said Grandma. "Go ahead and eat, Adam, and you'll grow up big and strong."

"Thank you, Grandma," said Adam. He hurried to his room and opened his book bag. The little dragon jumped out.

"Do you live here?" asked the little dragon. Adam nodded.

"What's that there?" asked the little dragon. "That thing that's so nice and warm?"

"A stove," said Adam. "Our house is old. We have real wood stoves with real fire."

"Fire?" sighed the little dragon. "Real fire? How nice!"

Adam opened the stove door. "My mother doesn't think it's so nice," he said. "She complains about the dirt and all the work."

But the little dragon puffed with happiness. "I'm so glad I met you," he said. "Quick, lift me up. I want to eat some fire. I'm starving."

Adam picked up the little dragon and held him up to the opening. The little dragon lapped and smacked and slurped and wagged his tail. It tasted so good!

"Don't you want to eat some fire?" he asked Adam.

"Fire?" Adam laughed. "People don't eat fire."

"What do you eat?" asked the little dragon.

"Spaghetti with tomato sauce," said Adam. "And chicken, and apple pie. And chocolate."

He took his chocolate bar and tore off the wrapper.

"My grandma gives me a bar almost every day. Sometimes two. And cake. And candy. Here, try a piece."

The little dragon shook his head. "Dragons eat only fire," he said and sniffed. "It smells good, though. Could you throw a piece in the fire for me? I'd love to try chocolate fire."

"Okay," said Adam. He opened the stove door and threw two pieces of chocolate onto the grate. They sizzled, and the little dragon gobbled them up.

"Hmmmm," he said. "Hmmmmmm! Good! I've never tasted such good fire in my whole life. Chocolate fire tastes terrific!"

"Now I'll have some," said Adam.

"Such a big piece?" asked the little dragon. "That's almost all of it!"

"But it's *my* chocolate," said Adam.

"Couldn't I have just a little bit more?" asked the little dragon.

"Oh, all right," said Adam and he tossed the piece into the stove.

"Lift me up!" puffed the little dragon. "Quick!"

Adam held him up to the opening and the

little dragon slurped and smacked and kept begging, again and again, "More, please, please more!" And he didn't stop until Adam had tossed the whole chocolate bar into the fire. There was nothing left for Adam. Not a single piece.

"It's all gone!" he said. "Oh well, grandma will give me more."

The little dragon licked his lips. "Good," he puffed. "Then I can eat chocolate fire every day. I'm lucky I met you." He stood up on his hind legs and began to hop and jump and spin in circles.

"What *are* you doing?" demanded Adam.

"Dancing!" said the little dragon. "This is a 'happy-dragon dance.' "

"Without music?" asked Adam.

"Music? What's that?" asked the little dragon.

Adam didn't know how he could explain it. So he made up a little song and he sang it to the little dragon:

> The little dragon loves to eat
> and fire is his favorite treat,
> but chocolate fire tastes so hot
> it makes the little dragon hop.

The little dragon put his head to one side and listened. "That sounds nice," he said. "Is that music?"

"It's called singing," said Adam.

"You sing very well," said the little dragon.

"Not really," said Adam. "I never sing in school. Larry Hall says I honk."

The little dragon blew a couple of small, dark clouds into the air. "This Larry Hall sounds stupid," he hissed. "Maybe he's hard of hearing. Please, sing it again for me."

Adam sang it again. By the third time, the little dragon was singing along with him:

> The little dragon loves to eat
> and fire is his favorite treat,
> but chocolate fire tastes so hot
> it makes the little dragon hop.

He sounded a bit hoarse and a bit scratchy, but the little dragon was very proud of his singing.

"I am the very first dragon to sing!" he puffed. "Me, with just one head! Come on, Adam, let's sing and dance."

"I don't know how to dance," said Adam. "I'm too fat."

"I don't believe *that*," said the little dragon. "You *sing* so beautifully."

Adam forgot that he was fat. He hopped behind the dragon and they sang the dragon song together.

Suddenly the door opened and Adam's mother came in.

"What is going on here?" she asked.

"I'm singing," said Adam. "And dancing, too!"

Adam's mother was pleased that Adam was so happy. She didn't see the little dragon. The little dragon belonged to Adam. And only Adam could see him.

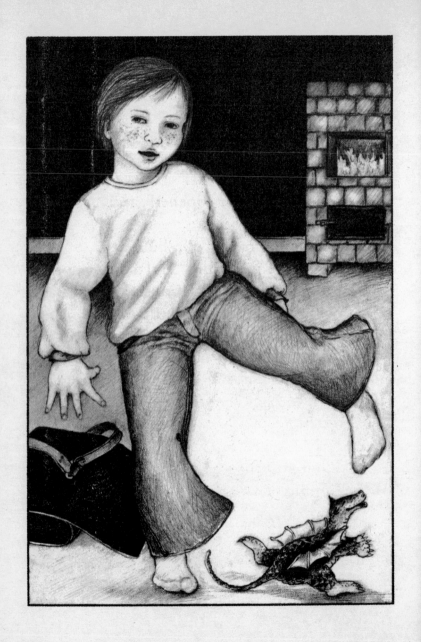

5. The Little Dragon Goes to School

The next morning, the little dragon crept into the book bag, and Adam took him to school with him.

"Move, Greasy Gravy!" said Larry Hall, shoving Adam against a desk.

"Shove him back," hissed the little dragon through a hole in the book bag. But Adam didn't dare.

"Take out your notebooks," said Mrs. Beck. "We are going to write."

The rabbit has long ears.

she wrote on the blackboard.

Adam bent over his notebook and wrote down the sentence. But he wasn't thinking of the rabbit with the long ears. He was thinking of Larry and Greasy Gravy. So all of his letters were crooked and lopsided, and every word was wrong.

During recess, Adam stayed by himself, away from the other kids, in a corner of the playground. He held his book bag close to his chest.

The little dragon stuck his head out and hissed, "That Larry is disgusting. He's just as disgusting as a couple of dragons in *my* class."

"Did you fight them back?" asked Adam.

"No," said the little dragon, "I didn't dare, either."

They both fell silent. After a while, the little dragon said, "But Larry isn't very bright. He said that you honk, and you sing so beautifully. I think he's *dumb*!"

The little dragon blew a small cloud into the air.

"Maybe he isn't strong at all," he said. "Maybe he just acts that way. Maybe if you fought back, he'd run away."

"I don't think so," said Adam.

"You could try," said the little dragon. "Then, I could try too. Later, when I go back home."

The bell rang. Recess was over. Adam went back to his classroom.

"Here comes Greasy Gravy!" yelled Larry Hall. Adam tried to pass him, but Larry shoved him again.

"Go ahead! Shove him back!" hissed the little dragon.

Adam lifted his book bag and slammed it against Larry. Larry tumbled back and sat down hard.

"Yeeow!" he yelled. "Tuba-Tummy shoved me! Yeeoww! My hand!"

Adam looked at Larry's friends. But not one of them moved. A couple of them even snickered, and Susie Vann said, "Well, *you* started it. You've been shoving Adam every day. It's about time he shoved you back."

Larry slunk back to his seat and didn't say another word.

6. The Little Dragon Learns to Write

The little dragon lay in front of the wood stove. He had just finished eating a lot of chocolate fire and was dozing.

But Adam couldn't rest, he had homework to do. He had to copy the sentence he had practiced at school: The rabbit has long ears.

The first time it read this way:

The rabit has log ears.

The second time, it looked like this:

The rbbit has lon ears.

And the third time, Adam wrote:

The rabbit hs long eas.

His mother looked at the notebook and shook her head. "Adam, this isn't right," she said. "Try again."

After she left, Adam just sat there, chewing on his pen. "I can't do it," he said loudly.

The little dragon opened his eyes. "What can't you do?" he asked.

"Do it right," said Adam.

The little dragon jumped up on top of the desk.

"How do you write, anyway?" he asked. "Show me."

Adam wrote

The rabbit

in his notebook.

"That's how," he said. "You should be glad you don't have to learn to write."

"It doesn't look hard at all," puffed the little dragon. "Do you have another one of these writing things?"

Adam gave him a pencil and a piece of paper.
"Now, show me again," said the little dragon.
Adam slowly drew one letter after another.
"That means, 'the rabbit,' " he said.

"The rabbit," repeated the little dragon, and
he, too, drew one letter after another on his
paper. "How does it look?"

"Crooked," said Adam. "You have to do it
this way."

And he wrote,

The rabbit

The little dragon tried to copy him. On his
third try, it looked better. "Go on," he said.
"The next word."

has wrote Adam.

has wrote the little dragon,
until it looked right.

Then, he learned how to write "long" and
"ears."

"Now, let's write it all down five times," puffed the little dragon. "Then we'll have it right."

The rabbit has long ears.

wrote Adam, once, twice, three, four, and five times. Just as he finished, his mother came into the room.

"Well done," she said. "Good work, Adam."

"What about me?" asked the little dragon when she left.

"You did well, too," said Adam.

The little dragon puffed with joy. He sat down on top of Adam's notebook, and he made up a song:

> The little dragon loves to write
> although his letters are a fright,
> and though it's true he's very small
> he'd love to write it on the wall. . . .

"Do you like my song?" he asked.

"It's not bad," said Adam.

The little dragon blew a small cloud into Adam's face.

"For a dragon," he puffed, "it's *very* good."

7. The Little Dragon Turns a Somersault

Adam and the little dragon were sitting on the bed. Adam scratched the little dragon's head while the little dragon told him about Dragonland. "I have a dragonmother and a dragondad and a dragongrandma and a dragongrandpa," he said. "My grandma . . ."

He stopped talking. Adam's grandma came into the room. She put a big piece of cake on the table. Crumb cake. Adam's favorite kind.

"I made it especially for you," she said.

The little dragon raised his head and sniffed.

"That smells good," he puffed. "Is that cake? I wonder if cake fire tastes good."

"The cake is mine," said Adam. "I'm going to eat it."

The little dragon puffed sadly. He nodded his head and wagged his tail and begged. So Adam ate only half. The rest he threw into the stove.

The little dragon slurped and smacked. "Hmmmmmmmm!" he said. "Cake fire tastes good, too. I'll have to sing a cake fire song."

He and Adam sang together:

> The little dragon loves to eat
> and fire is his favorite treat
> but crumbcake fire tastes so cool
> it makes the little dragon drool.

"Now tell me more about Dragonland," said Adam.

The little dragon thought. "Once a year, we have a big fire festival," he said. "All the little dragons have fire-breathing contests. I always lose because I have only one head."

"I always lose, too," said Adam. "I can't run. I can't play ball or turn somersaults. Larry Hall can do ten somersaults in a row. I can barely do one."

"What's a somersault?" asked the little dragon.

Adam turned a somersault. It wasn't a very good one, but the little dragon laughed.

"I want to do that, too," he said. He tucked his head down, stuck his tail in the air, and flopped onto his side.

"That was not so good," he puffed.

Adam had to show him again. And then a third and a fourth time. Finally, the little dragon knew how to do a perfect somersault.

"Now I want to do three in a row," he said. "Just like you, Adam."

"Me?" stammered Adam. "I can't do that!"

"You just did," said the little dragon. "I saw you. Come on, do it again."

So Adam did what the little dragon asked. And he really could do it! Three somersaults!

"Now me!" puffed the little dragon.

Adam and the little dragon tried and tried until they could turn *four* somersaults in a row.

"Four somersaults!" puffed the little dragon. "Four! I'm the only dragon in the world who can do that!"

He waggled his head, blew a small cloud into the air, and looked at Adam.

"This has been a great day," he said. "Cake fire! Somersaults! I'm lucky to have you!"

8. The Little Dragon Draws a Picture

Adam had a new box of crayons. Big, beautiful color crayons. But he wasn't happy about them.

"What are they?" asked the little dragon. He sniffed at the box. "Can you eat them?"

"No," said Adam. "You draw with them. Color drawings." He pointed at the drawing over his bed. It was a picture of two fish, a red one and a blue one.

"I drew that last year," he said.

"You draw beautifully," said the little dragon.

"Not anymore," said Adam. "Larry Hall says my pictures are stupid. Nothing but blobs."

The little dragon looked at the fish drawing. Then he looked at the crayons. Finally he said, "I want to draw. Please show me how."

"No," said Adam. "I don't draw anymore. Let's play instead."

The little dragon crept up to Adam and rubbed his head against Adam's leg. "I really want to draw," he begged. "Please teach me!"

"You are such a pest!" grumbled Adam. But he went and got his pad of drawing paper and scribbled some squiggles and smudges.

The little dragon took a crayon and copied Adam. "That's not a pretty drawing," he puffed. "Show me how to do pretty drawings."

"I can't!" said Adam angrily, but finally he gave in. "What should I draw?" he asked.

"Me," puffed the little dragon.

Adam looked the little dragon up and down. "I'm going to draw you in red," he said. "Because you're so cheerful."

Adam took his red crayon and drew the head, the stomach, the back, and the tongue.

"Do I look like *that*?" asked the little dragon. "Do I really?"

"A little," said Adam. "I guess it's not really very good."

The little dragon sat on his haunches and took a crayon and began to draw too: first, a small round circle; then a big, fat circle with two lines on either side.

"That's *you*," he said. "Do you like my drawing?"

"It's a good beginning," said Adam, "but you forgot my legs."

"Well, you forgot mine," said the little dragon. "Now let's draw until we each make a good drawing. Do you want to?"

"Not really," said Adam. But because the little dragon wanted to so much, Adam gave in.

They drew all afternoon. Adam forgot that he didn't like to draw. He and the little dragon drew many bright pictures, each nicer than the one before. They hung the two best ones over Adam's bed. Adam's drawing was of the little dragon sitting in front of the stove and gobbling chocolate fire. The little dragon's drawing was of Adam throwing cake into the wood stove.

"We are both great artists!" puffed the little dragon.

Adam nodded. "Larry Hall would be surprised," he said.

"So would the dragons at home," puffed the little dragon. "Hey! What are you doing? Don't eat that chocolate without me!"

9. The Little Dragon Climbs a Tree

Adam and the little dragon were playing tag in the garden. The little dragon had short legs, but he could run very fast. Adam had to run hard to tag him. At first, he often missed. But now he was getting better at it and the little dragon had to run faster to get away from Adam.

"I can't run anymore," gasped the little dragon. He flopped down under the apple tree.

Adam sat down beside him. The sun was bright. Winter was almost over.

"It's a tall tree," said the little dragon. "Can you see far from the top of it?"

"I don't know," said Adam. "I have never climbed it."

"Why not?" asked the little dragon.

Adam didn't answer. He was afraid the little dragon would want to climb the tree.

"Let's go inside," Adam said.

The little dragon grabbed Adam firmly by the pant leg. "Please," he hissed, "show me how to climb. I want to sit high up in the tree. I want to tell the other dragons about it."

"But I don't know how to climb," said Adam.

"I don't believe it," said the little dragon. "That sounds like something Larry Hall would say. He is always saying something stupid. Let's climb up!"

Slowly, very slowly, Adam stood up. He grabbed hold of a branch; he braced his feet firmly against the trunk, and pulled himself up. The little dragon watched carefully. Then he climbed up after him. "So far, so good," he puffed. "We'll make it to the top."

They climbed from branch to branch. Adam panted and groaned and grumbled. The little dragon panted, too. Finally they reached the top. They could see the whole garden, and the street beyond, and even onto the porch of the next-door neighbors. Mrs. Bergman was out poking around in her garden.

The little dragon blew thick clouds of smoke into the air.

"I'm king of the dragons!" he boasted. "Me! The smallest dragon! Me! The only dragon with one head! When I tell them about this in Drag-onland, they'll never pick on me again!"

Then the little dragon looked down and gulped.

"We're up high, " he said.

"Very high," said Adam.

"How are we going to get down?" asked the little dragon.

"I don't know," said Adam.

"I'm scared," puffed the little dragon.

"I am too," said Adam.

The little dragon began to cry. Great big tears. "I'll n-n-never get d-d-down from here," he sobbed. "I'll n-n-never eat any more choc-olate f-f-fire."

The little dragon was crying so loudly that Adam couldn't bear it. He tucked him inside his pocket. "Don't cry," said Adam, "I'm going to try to get us down."

But it was no use. The tree was too tall and Adam was too afraid.

They sat there until Adam's father came home and helped Adam climb down.

"Step down onto that branch," he said. "Hold tight! Now the next, over there. Don't be afraid, you're *almost* down. There now! Next time you want to climb up a tree, remember that you must also climb down!"

Adam nodded. He had had enough of tree climbing. But the little dragon soon forgot he had been crying.

"Climbing is fun!" he exclaimed. "Let's do it again tomorrow!"

10. The Little Dragon Reads a Story

By now, the little dragon had been with Adam for quite a while. He played with Adam. He slept at the foot of his bed. And every day he gobbled chocolate fire. He had learned many things: singing, dancing, turning somersaults, climbing trees. Now the little dragon wanted to learn how to read.

"No," said Adam. "Reading is boring. It takes at least an hour to get through one page."

"Not your grandma," said the little dragon.

"Well, she knows *how*," said Adam.

"You have a big, bright book on your shelf," said the little dragon. "What is in it?"

"Stories," said Adam.

"Stories like the ones your grandma sometimes reads to you?" asked the little dragon.

Adam nodded.

The little dragon puffed out a small, round cloud. "I want to be a dragon who can read stories," he said.

Once the little dragon had made up his mind to do something, he gave Adam no rest. When they went for a walk, the little dragon stopped in front of every poster and store sign and asked, "What letter is that? What is that word? Read it to me, *now!*"

Soon the little dragon could read many difficult words. DRUGSTORE. LAUNDROMAT. SUPERMARKET. TOOTHPASTE. CLEANING. So one day, Adam took the storybook down from the shelf.

"What does this say?" the little dragon asked and pointed with his right front claw at the first page.

"Read it yourself," said Adam.

The little dragon sat down in Adam's lap. "The Bre-bre-brem . . ."

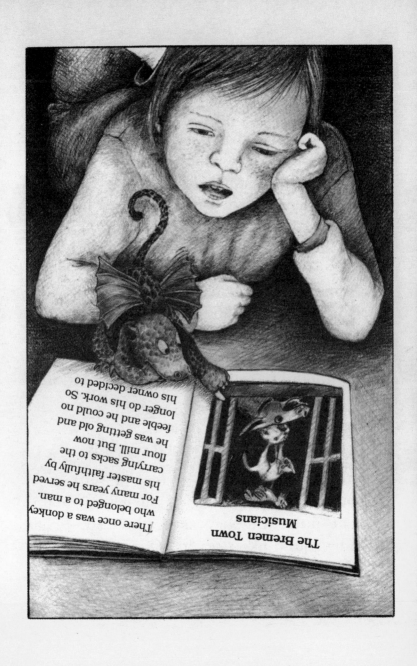

The Bremen Town
Musicians

There once was a donkey
who belonged to a man.
For many years he served
his master faithfully by
carrying sacks to the
flour mill. But now
he was getting old and
feeble and he could no
longer do his work. So
his owner decided to

"That's 'The Bremen,' " said Adam. "The Bremen Town Mu-musicians."

"Go on!" said the little dragon. "The Bremen Town Musicians."

They began to read the story together. It was a good story. They liked it so much they didn't stop until they had read two pages.

"Reading is hard work," groaned the little dragon. "My head aches. Does yours?"

"A little," said Adam.

"How long did it take us to read two pages?" asked the little dragon.

"Half an hour," said Adam.

"We can read fast," puffed the little dragon. "I will make up a song now."

He thought a while and began:

> The little dragon loves to read;
> they said he couldn't do it; . . .
> but now they'll have to eat their words . . .

"I don't know how to go on," he puffed.

"And Adam will see to it," suggested Adam.

The little dragon cocked his head. "That doesn't sound like *you*," he said.

"Maybe," said Adam, "maybe not."

11. Summer Begins

"Wake up, Adam," said Mother. "It's time for school."

Adam yawned. The little dragon yawned, too. Adam scratched the little dragon's back, then walked to the bathroom. He brushed his teeth and took his bath. He played boats with the soap dish.

Outside, the sun was shining. Adam put on his short pants.

"Summer is almost here," his mother said at breakfast. "We don't have to keep those wood stoves going anymore."

The little dragon was waiting for Adam in

his book bag. They crossed the street, walked through the park, across the school yard, and into Adam's classroom.

"Tuba-Tummy!" called Larry Hall.

Adam didn't pay any attention to him. That annoyed Larry.

"Greasy Gravy," called Larry.

"Larry Hall, dumb as a wall!" answered Adam.

"That's a good one!" puffed the little dragon and he laughed loudly. The other children laughed too.

"Larry Hall's dumb, that's all!" Susie Vann chimed in. "He can't even see that Adam hasn't *got* a tuba-tummy anymore."

"And he can run a lot faster than before," added Steve Stark.

Mrs. Beck came in and said, "Take out your books. We are going to read."

Susie Vann was first. Adam was next. He read five sentences and made only two mistakes.

"Good work, Adam!" said Mrs. Beck, and Adam was happy. He could read. He no longer

had a tuba-tummy. School was much nicer now.

At recess, Susie Vann came up to Adam.

"My birthday is on Friday, Adam," she said. "I'm having a party and I want you to come. Andy Hoffman and Steve Stark and Annette Steinbaum and George Miller and Sabina Smith are coming, too."

That made Adam even happier. He thought hard about what he could give Susie for her birthday. It would have to be something very special.

"I'm here, Adam!" puffed the little dragon. He peeked out of Adam's jacket pocket and blew a cloud into the air. Adam scratched him.

"I know," said Adam. But he was thinking about the birthday party.

12. Adam Is No Longer Alone

School was over. Adam and the little dragon were walking through the park toward home. When they came to the bench near the beech tree, Adam sat down. The little dragon jumped out of his book bag and lay down at Adam's feet.

"Last night I dreamed of Dragonland again," he said.

"What did you dream about?" asked Adam.

"I dreamed about my mother and my father," said the little dragon. "I dreamed about my dragon school. I even dreamed I turned somersaults and sang, and all the other dragons were very impressed."

"Really?" asked Adam.

The little dragon nodded.

"It was a nice dream," he said softly. Adam and the little dragon sat there. They did not say a word.

"Are we going home, soon?" asked the little dragon. "I'm hungry. What's for supper? Chocolate fire or cake fire?"

"Neither," said Adam. "Winter is over. My mother won't be burning wood in the stoves anymore now."

"Wh-what?" stammered the little dragon. "That's terrible!"

"And my grandma won't give me any more chocolate or cake," said Adam. "She saw me throwing them into the fire."

The little dragon blew a pair of thick clouds into the air. He laid his head down on his front claws and sighed heavily.

"Let's go home," said Adam. The little dragon didn't move.

"Let's go," said Adam again.

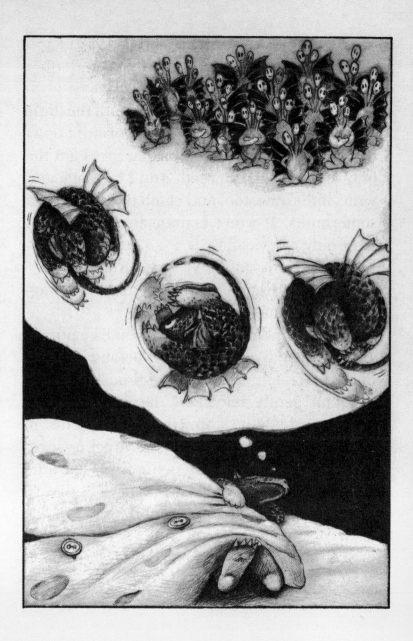

The little dragon raised his head.

"No," he said softly.

"What's wrong?" asked Adam.

"I'm not coming with you," said the little dragon. "I'm going home to Dragonland. I don't think anyone there is still mad at me. I am the only dragon who can read. And I can sing, and write, and draw, too, and climb trees, and turn somersaults. It won't matter, anymore, that I have only one head."

"Please don't go away," cried Adam.

The little dragon looked at Adam. He waggled his tail and blinked his eyes.

"It was wonderful to be with you," he puffed softly, "but I'm a dragon and I belong in Dragonland. Scratch me one more time."

Adam gently scratched the little dragon's head. Suddenly he stopped and looked down. There was no sign of the little dragon—only lines and circles scratched in the sand. The little dragon had disappeared!

"Little dragon!" cried Adam.

No one answered.

Sadly, very sadly, Adam walked home through

the park and across the street. The little dragon was no longer in his book bag.

On the corner Adam noticed a new store. A polished seashell lay in the store window.

Adam stood there staring at the seashell.

That's a beautiful seashell, Adam thought. I'll give that to Susie for her birthday.